CHRISTMAS TROLLS

Written and illustrated by

JAN BRETT

PUFFIN BOOKS

To Ashley, Abbie, Robby, and Mollie

PUFFIN BOOKS

Published by the Penguin Group

Penguin Putnam Books for Young Readers, 345 Hudson Street, New York, New York 10014, U.S.A.

Penguin Books Ltd, Registered Offices: Harmondsworth, Middlesex, England

First published in the United States of America by G. P. Putnam's Sons,
a division of The Putnam & Grosset Group, 1993
Published by Puffin Books, a division of Penguin Putnam Books for Young Readers, 2000

1 3 5 7 9 10 8 6 4 2

THE LIBRARY OF CONGRESS HAS CATALOGED THE G. P. PUTNAM'S SONS EDITION AS FOLLOWS:
Brett, Jan, date Christmas trolls/ Jan Brett. p. cm.
Summary: When Treva investigates the disappearance of her family's Christmas things,
she finds two mischievous trolls who have never had a Christmas of their own.
[1. Christmas—Fiction. 2. Trolls—Fiction.] I. Title.
PZ7.B7559.Ch 1993 [E]--dc20 93-10106 CIP AC
ISBN 0-399-22507-2

Puffin Books ISBN 0-698-11846-4

Airbrush backgrounds by Joseph Hearne
Text set in Garamond #3
Lettering by David Gatti

Printed in the United States of America

I'm Treva, and the day my brother Sami and I went to our neighbor's farm to pick out a Christmas tree was the beginning of the most unforgettable Christmas I ever had.

As we went home through the forest with a perfect tree packed on the sleigh, Tuffi started sniffing and barking. I couldn't see anything, but I felt sure someone was watching us.

When we arrived home, we forgot all about the forest. Mom and
Dad had brought out our boxes of ornaments to decorate the tree.
Sami and I put evergreen wreaths, mistletoe and holly all around
the house. We had already wrapped our presents and hidden them
away for Christmas morning.

Then some of our Christmas decorations started to disappear.
I didn't notice until Dad asked if we had moved the trinket box
he had hidden for Mom. I shivered because Mom had just asked
me the same thing about the mittens she had knitted for Dad.

Sami and I looked in all the usual hiding places, but we couldn't find them. Tuffi was acting strange too. He sniffed and barked and ran around in circles as if he were looking for something.

Then a few days before Christmas, the treetop angel was gone. What would be next? I started carrying my favorite red horse everywhere.

Early the next morning when I went to feed Arni, I saw
something flying across the snow. It was our Christmas pudding!

I harnessed Arni, bells and all, and raced after it into the forest.
As I got closer, I could see that our pudding was being carried
along, pincushioned to the top of a hedgehog. I didn't know what
to do, so I yelled, "Stop! Come back."

But it didn't stop until it reached the bottom of four fir trees.
The hedgehog put the pudding down and scampered off. Just then
the trees started rocking back and forth.

Suddenly a funny-looking ladder dropped down from above, and two trolls scurried down, pouncing on the pudding before I could even move. They pulled it back and forth as they went up the ladder, squabbling all the way to the top.

I climbed right up after them and looked inside.
There on the floor of their troll house were all of our
Christmas things in a heap. The trolls were grabbing
at them, each one wanting what the other one had.

"Hey, trolls!" I called. "Those are our Christmas things!" The trolls dove onto the pile, clutching our gifts. "Mine," they clamored. "Mine! Mine!"

I looked at them and had to smile. Their shirttails were hanging out. Their pants were torn and patched. Their cheeks were bright red and their hair was standing straight up from all the pulling and tugging at each other.

"Christmas!" they wailed. "We want Christmas!"

"You want Christmas?" I asked, puzzled.

"Yes!" they shouted. "Give us Christmas!"

"Well, you can't just take Christmas," I said.

The trolls looked surprised. They squeaked. They gulped. They shuffled their feet.

"Want Christmas," they said, sounding miserable.

"Okay, you can have Christmas. But first, what are your names?"
"Mig," said one.
"Tig," said the other.
I looked around their messy hut.

"Mig, Tig, let's begin by getting your house ready for Christmas." I started to straighten up and put things away. They began to help.

"Nice," I said when we had finished. "Now let's make your house look like Christmas."

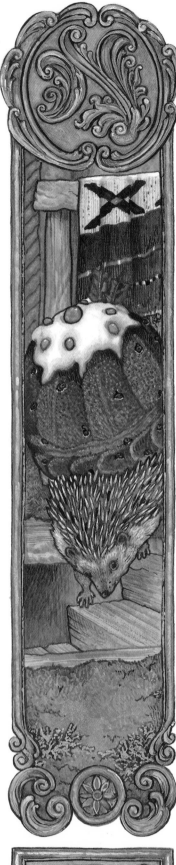

We went outside and gathered evergreens, berries and pinecones. "Now we need a Christmas tree," I told them. "That's easy. You live in the trees, so you can have four trees instead of just one if you want to."

"Christmas trees!" they shouted, jumping up and down, and we decorated each of the trees that held up the troll house.

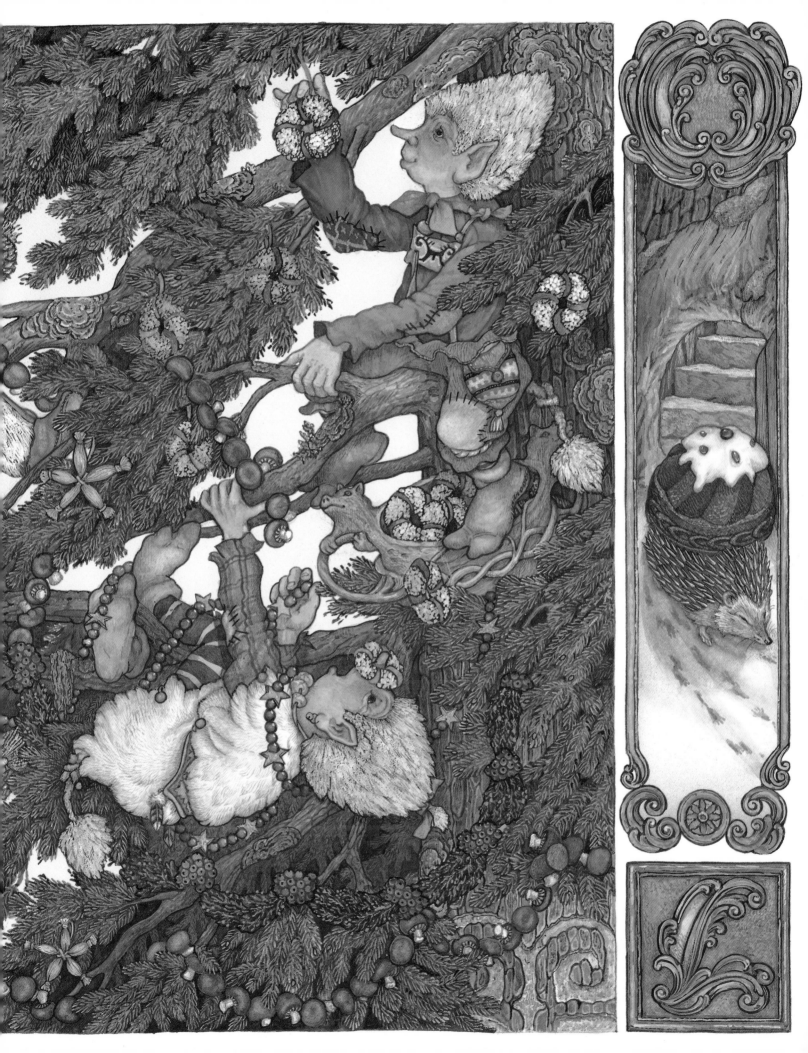

Tig and Mig had a small setback on the way back to the hut. I knew I had some more explaining to do. "When I first got here, you were snatching things for yourselves and acting really grumpy. Try playing together and having some fun."

"Fun?" they asked.

I showed them how to jump rope. I told them how much I liked their tail knots and earrings. They smiled shyly and started tucking in their shirttails.

"Nice hair. Pretty belt," they said, grinning at me. And they taught me a little troll dance. They were catching on.

"Now if you really want Christmas, you must be generous with each other. If you do that, you will have Christmas right here in your troll house."

The trolls cocked their heads and squinted. They were trying hard to understand. "How?" they pleaded.

I felt my red horse in my pocket. I knew I had to show them, so I took it out and gave it to them.

"This is for you."

The trolls squealed and jumped up and down with glee. They took turns passing my horse back and forth, happily playing with it together. It was time for me to go home.

I slipped out quietly and climbed down to Arni. To my surprise,
their hedgehog had packed all of our presents on the sleigh, for me
to take home, while we were having Christmas in the troll house.

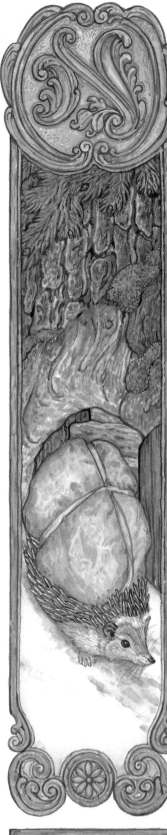

On Christmas morning, Sami and I ran downstairs to find our tree alight with candles and our stockings filled. We opened our presents in front of the fire.

But this Christmas was full of surprises. I heard a bumping and a scratching noise. Tuffi barked. I listened and followed the sounds. Outside on the doorstep was a Christmas present.

I unwrapped it and found a wild and wonderful troll horse.
"Tig and Mig!" I exclaimed.
When I held it, I knew for sure that the trolls understood
Christmas and I knew that this was the best Christmas ever.